The Adventures of Sunny & The Chocolate Dog

Sunny & The Chocolate Dog Go to the Doctor

Written by Susie Neimark
Illustrated by Kent Hammerstrom

Printed in Canada

ISBN# 0-9725945-2-3
LCCN# 2002095834

Written by Susie Neimark
Cover design & illustration by Kent Hammerstrom

Sunny & The Chocolate Dog, LLC
5 Palm Row, Suite C
St. Augustine, FL 32084

This book is dedicated to Ken, Sharon, Donna, Jeffrey, Philip, Vassa, Linda, Joe and Dr. Kathleen Deckard, DVM

May the happiness and love Sunny & Cloudy have shown us be shared and enjoyed by many others.

Special thanks to Kathy Tanaka, Tanya Husain, Kathleen Rowan, Courtney Goes, Johanna Hannah and, of course, Sunny & Cloudy (The Chocolate Dog) for the inspiration they have provided.

Today was the perfect day, warm and breezy. From the moment Sunny and Cloudy got out of bed, they knew it was a perfect day to go to the park. They gazed out the window at the beautiful day and thought about all of the fun they would have playing fetch with their red ball and chasing squirrels. Sunny and Cloudy ran downstairs to ask their mommy when they could get started.

Sunny picked up her favorite red ball and dropped it at her mommy's feet. This was Sunny's way of reminding her mommy that today would be a perfect day to go the park. Their mommy agreed, it was a perfect day to go to the park and play, but, sadly, they would not be able to go today. "Why not?" asked Sunny.

Sunny and Cloudy did not understand. They always went to the park on perfect days like this one. "I am very sorry girls, but today we are all going to take a trip to see the doctor for a checkup," said their mommy. "Doctor? Checkup? What's that?" asked Cloudy.

Sunny had been going to the doctor since she was a puppy, but this was going to be Cloudy's first visit. Sunny was not very happy to hear that it was going to be a doctor day instead of a park day. Cloudy wasn't very happy to hear this news either, but she still didn't understand what a doctor day was. Sunny put her head on her mommy's lap and looked up at her with her biggest, saddest, puppy dog eyes. "We don't need to visit the doctor, Mom. We feel fine," said Sunny.

Cloudy noticed how concerned Sunny was about going to this doctor place, and this made her a little scared. In a flash, Cloudy ran to her basket of toys, grabbed her green froggy, jumped into her bed, and buried her head beneath her paws. Sunny saw how frightened Cloudy was and walked over to where she was hiding to try to make her little sister feel better.

"Don't worry, little sis. It's not that bad," said Sunny. She explained to Cloudy that the doctor's office was not her favorite place to go either, but it was something that they had to do to stay healthy. Cloudy still wasn't happy about going, no matter what Sunny told her.

"Come on, Sunny and Cloudy! It's time to go visit the doctor," shouted their mommy. The time had come for the girls and their mommy to take a ride to the doctor's office for their checkup. Cloudy did not want to get in the car, so her mommy told her that she could bring her green froggy along if that would make her feel better.

Sunny was already in the backseat, and she was trying to think of a way to encourage Cloudy to get in. Then she got an idea! Sunny told Cloudy about the special dog treats they would get at the doctor's office. "They are special because they are different from the kind of treats we get at home," explained Sunny. Sunny had said the magic word — TREATS. Cloudy dashed over and plopped herself in the backseat next to Sunny.

The thought of a special, different kind of treat made Cloudy feel a little bit better because she loved getting treats. Now Cloudy was a little more willing to go to the doctor's office, but only because she wanted to try these new mysterious treats.

Before long, they arrived at the doctor's office. Sunny got out of the car, but Cloudy was too frightened to follow her. Sunny reminded Cloudy about the special treats and told her that the sooner she got out, the sooner she could have one. It took a little bit of convincing, but Cloudy finally decided to get out of the car and go inside with Sunny and her mommy.

After checking in at the front desk, Sunny showed Cloudy where they could play with toys and games while they waited for the doctor. "Where are the treats?" Cloudy asked. Sunny told her that they could not get a treat until after their checkup. Cloudy didn't like this news. She would have rather had the treat now and not have to see the doctor at all.

Suddenly, the door opened, and the doctor walked out wearing a white coat. With a soft, friendly voice she said, "Hello there, Sunny! It is so nice to see you again!" Then the doctor looked over at Cloudy and said, "And, hello to you too! You must be Cloudy. It's so very nice to meet Sunny's baby sister!" Sunny greeted the doctor with a big smile. Cloudy, on the other hand, was still a little unsure about all of this.

Now it was time to follow the doctor into the checkup room. Cloudy felt a little bit better after meeting the friendly doctor in the waiting room, but she was starting to get nervous all over again. She didn't know what was going to happen next. Her mommy and Sunny noticed how frightened Cloudy was, so they tried to comfort her with some hugs and reminded her, once again, about the special treats.

The doctor examined Sunny first so that Cloudy could watch before it was her turn. First, the doctor put Sunny up on the examination table and checked to make sure her bones, muscles, and coat of fur felt normal and healthy. Cloudy hid under a chair the whole time Sunny was being checked, but she peeked her head out and carefully watched what the doctor was doing.

The doctor took out a strange instrument called a stethoscope and placed it on Sunny's chest to listen to her heart. Then the doctor placed the stethoscope on Sunny's back to listen to her lungs, and she told Sunny to take a deep breath. Sunny whispered over to Cloudy, "This doesn't hurt at all." Next, the doctor took out a thermometer to take Sunny's temperature to make sure that she didn't have a fever. "So far, so good, Sunny," said the doctor.

All that was left for the doctor to do was to give Sunny her shot. The doctor explained that shots were very important for Sunny and Cloudy because they helped protect the girls from germs that were all around, especially outdoors. This was Sunny's least favorite part about visiting the doctor because it hurt just a little bit, like a pinch. "Oh dear! I can't look!" Cloudy sighed, as she covered her eyes.

The doctor gently cleaned a little area on Sunny's arm and then filled a small needle with a medicine called a vaccine. The doctor told Sunny that it would be done by the time she counted to three. Sunny shut her eyes and counted out loud, "One, two, three." When she opened her eyes, the doctor was all done!

"Okay, Sunny, you are all done. Thank you for being such a good patient!" said the doctor. She took a special treat out of a jar and gave it to Sunny. As soon as Cloudy saw the treat, she popped her head out from under the chair. "Can I have one too?" she asked. The doctor told Cloudy that she could have one just as soon as they were done with the examination.

Now it was Cloudy's turn. Gulp! Cloudy didn't want to come out from under the chair. Her mommy told her that she didn't need to be afraid and reminded her how brave Sunny was during her examination and how Cloudy could be brave too. "Don't forget about the special treat," said Sunny. Slowly, Cloudy crawled out from under the chair, and the doctor gently lifted her up onto the table.

"Okay Cloudy, I promise that this isn't going to hurt a bit. Everything is going to be fine," said the doctor. The doctor made especially sure to speak to Cloudy very gently. She started doing all the same tests on Cloudy that she did with Sunny. She carefully examined Cloudy's bones and felt her muscles and her coat. "So far, so good, Cloudy," said the doctor.

"Now it's time to listen to your heart and lungs," said the doctor. Cloudy remembered when the doctor did this to Sunny and how it didn't look like it had hurt at all. Cloudy took a deep breath, and the doctor listened through her stethoscope. "Sounds perfect," said the doctor. Next, the doctor brought out the thermometer. The doctor placed it in Cloudy's mouth. Her temperature was just right!

Now it was time for the part that Cloudy was most worried about - the shot. "Okay Cloudy, we are almost finished. All we have left to do is give you the vaccine," said the doctor. This news made Cloudy very nervous, but she tried to only think about the treat she would get afterward. Cloudy shut her eyes tightly, as she snuggled next to her mommy who hugged her right back. Sunny stayed right next to her the entire time too.

The doctor told Cloudy that she would feel a little pinch, just like Sunny did. Oh dear! Cloudy was so scared she could barely breathe. "Oh Mommy! Please don't let the doctor give me a shot! PLEASE!" begged Cloudy. She had just begun to cry when all of a sudden she heard the doctor say, "Okay Cloudy, you are all done! Here is your treat." "All done?" asked Cloudy as she opened up her eyes. "But, it didn't even hurt!"

As Sunny and Cloudy left the doctor's office, their mommy congratulated them both for being so brave. "I am so proud of my girls!" said their mommy. "And guess what else? There is still time to go to the park and play fetch before dinner!" Well, Sunny and Cloudy woofed with excitement and gave each other high-fives! Cloudy thought for a moment, and then turned to her mommy and said, "This going to the doctor business isn't so bad after all."

Join the Sunny & The Chocolate Dog Pen Pal Club!!!

How many dogs do you know who have their very own email address?
Well, Sunny and Cloudy do!
One of their favorite things to do is to write to their friends, so email them a
message or a question, and they will write back!
If you are a pen pal, Sunny and Cloudy will also tell you when they have gone on
a new adventure so that you can read all about it.

Sunny and Cloudy even have their own website with fun facts, puzzles and games
too!

Visit Sunny and The Chocolate Dog at: www.sunnyandthechocolatedog.com

Go on another adventure with Sunny & The Chocolate Dog

Sunny Meets Her Baby Sister
ISBN# 0-9725945-0-7

Sunny & The Chocolate Dog Go to the Beach
ISBN# 0-9725945-1-5